The Lucky Baseball Bat

by Matt Christopher

Illustrated by Dee deRosa

SPRINGBOARD
B·O·O·K·S

Little, Brown and Company
Boston   Toronto   London

The Lucky
Baseball Bat

This is a revised edition of *The Lucky Baseball Bat* published in
1954 by Little, Brown and Company.

The characters and events portrayed in this book are fictitious.
Any similarity to real persons, living or dead, is coincidental
and not intended by the author.

Christopher, Matt.
  The lucky baseball bat/by Matt Christopher; illustrated by
Dee deRosa. — Rev. ed.
    p.   cm. — (A Springboard book)
  Summary: When Martin loses his lucky baseball bat, and his
  confidence along with it, he wonders if he will recover both
  in time to help the Tigers win the championship.
  ISBN 0-316-14073-2
  [1. Baseball — Fiction.   2. Self-confidence —
  Fiction.]   I. deRosa, Dee, ill.   II. Title.
PZ7.C458Lu   1991
[E] — dc20   90-19188

Springboard Books and design is a trademark of Little, Brown
and Company (Inc.)

10 9 8 7 6 5 4 3 2 1

WOR

*Published simultaneously in Canada
by Little, Brown & Company (Canada) Limited*

PRINTED IN THE UNITED STATES OF AMERICA

To Marty, Pam, Dale, and Duane

1

Martin bit his lip and wiped his damp forehead with the back of his hand. His younger sister, Jeannie, scowled at him.

"What're you afraid of? Go in there and ask them," she said.

"Ask who?" Martin said.

He looked at the group of boys scattered on the ball field. They were practicing, throwing the ball among themselves to limber up their muscles and get the feel of it.

Jeannie brushed a tangle of curly hair away from her eyes and pointed. "Ask that man there. Jim Cassell. He's the coach, I think."

Martin didn't want to ask Jim Cassell. Mr. Cassell might tell him to go home. He didn't know Martin, and Martin didn't know him. That was the trouble. Martin knew hardly anybody here. They had just moved into the city.

"I think I'll just go out there with those kids and see if they'll throw a ball to me," he said. "That'll be all right, won't it?"

Jeannie nodded. "Go ahead. Maybe it's the best way."

Martin ran slowly toward the scattered group of boys. They were all about his age, some a little smaller, some taller. Most of them had baseball gloves. He wished he had one. You didn't look like a baseball player without a baseball glove.

All at once he heard Coach Cassell yell:

"Okay, boys! Spread out! A couple of you get in center field!"

The boys scampered into different positions, but Martin didn't move from the position he'd taken in left field. Coach Cassell was having the boys start batting practice. A tall, skinny kid stood on the mound. He pitched the ball twice. Each time, the boy at bat swung at the ball and missed.

The third time he connected. Martin heard the sharp *crack!* It was followed by a scramble of feet not far behind him. He looked up, and sure enough the ball, looking like a small white pill, was curving through the air in his direction!

"I got it! I got it!" he cried. He forgot that he had no glove. His sneakers slipped on the short-cut grass as he tried to get in position under the ball.

Somebody bumped into him, but he didn't give ground. "I got it!" he yelled again.

The ball came directly at him, and he reached for it with both hands. In the next instant the hurtling ball became a blur, and he felt it slide through his hands and strike solidly against his chest.

Missed it!

"Nice catch!" a boy sneered. "Where did you learn to play ball?"

2

"For Pete's sake!" the coach yelled. "Don't try to catch a ball without a glove! You'll get hurt!"

Martin looked at his bare hands, feeling his heart pound in his chest. He turned and walked away, sticking his hands in his pockets. "Come on," he said when he reached Jeannie. "Let's go home."

"Sure," Jeannie agreed. "You can do something else besides play baseball!"

"But I don't want to do anything else!" Martin said angrily. "I want to play baseball!"

"Hello!" a voice cut in as Martin and Jeannie started to walk off the field. "What's the matter, kid? You look as if you've lost your best friend."

Martin looked around at a tall, dark-haired boy standing behind them. "Nothing's the matter," he answered. He kept walking, his heels scraping the dirt and pebbles.

"Hey, wait a minute!" the tall stranger called after them. "You didn't answer me. What happened? Won't they let you play ball with them?"

"I haven't got a glove," Martin explained. "I'm sure I could catch those balls if I had a glove."

The tall boy laughed in a friendly way. "Tell you what," he said. "My name's Barry Welton. I live around the corner on Grant Street, to the right."

"We live a block to the left," Jeannie said warmly. "I'm Jeannie Allan, and this is my brother Martin."

"Glad to meet you. Now come on." He made a motion with his hand and began to walk toward Grant Street.

"Where are you going?" Martin asked.

"To my house. I'm going to give you something. Something I think you'd like to have."

When they reached Barry's house, a gray wood-frame building with yellow shutters, he asked them to wait in the living room while he ran upstairs. A few seconds later he was back, and Martin's eyes almost bugged out of his head.

Barry was carrying a bat and a glove!

"Here." He grinned. "These are yours. Now maybe they'll let you play. Okay?"

"Wow!" Martin cried. "You're giving these to me?"

"Right! I've had that glove ever since I was your size, and I outgrew that bat years ago. It was a lucky bat for me. Maybe it'll be a lucky one for you, too."

8

"Wow!" said Martin again, his heart thumping excitedly. "Thanks! Thanks a lot, Barry!" He turned to his sister. "Come on, Jeannie! Let's go back to the park!"

The kids were still having batting practice. Martin had Jeannie hang on to the bat while he put on the glove and ran out to the field. Two of the boys saw him with the glove and said something to each other. He acted as if he didn't see them. He didn't care what they said. He had as much right to be here as they did.

Suddenly he saw Jim Cassell gazing toward the outfield. The coach seemed to be looking directly at him, and Martin's heart fell.

"Kid!" the coach yelled at him. "Move over a little — toward center field!"

A thrill of excitement went through him as he ran over to a spot between left and center fields. The coach had given him an order as if he were already a member of the team! He almost prayed a ball would come his way. He had not caught a ball since last summer, but he knew how to do it. Maybe he could even show the kids a thing or two!

And then, even while he was thinking about it, he saw a ball hit out his way. The closer of the two boys covering center field came running for it, shouting at the top of his lungs, "I've got it! I've got it!"

Martin knew it was his ball more than the other boy's. He needed to take only four or five steps backward. He reached up — and tried to out-yell the other boy.

"It's mine! Let it go! It's mine!"

"Let him take it, Tommy!" Coach Cassell's voice boomed from near home plate.

Martin felt a shoulder hit his arm. It threw him off balance enough so that the ball struck the fingers of his glove and slipped right through. *Bang!* On his chest again, barely missing his throat. The ball dropped to the grass and bounced away.

Martin turned, tears choking him. He saw

that the other fielder was the same boy who had made a nasty remark earlier.

"So it's you again," the boy said. "With a glove, too!" He laughed. "Even with a glove you miss them. Why don't you go home and stay there? We don't want any hicks on this team!"

3

This time when Martin and Jeannie went home, there was no Barry Welton around. Martin was glad Barry had not seen how foolish he had looked on the diamond.

"I'm glad you're home, kids," their mother said. "We're almost ready for supper."

Then she caught sight of the bat and glove Martin was carrying. "Where on earth did you get those?" she asked.

"A nice guy named Barry Welton gave them to me," Martin said, then told his mother what had happened.

The basement door opened and Martin's tall, husky father came in. He stared at the bat and glove, too, and Martin had to tell all about it again. He left out one thing, though. He didn't tell them he was going to give the bat and glove back to Barry.

After supper Martin and Jeannie cleared the table and put the dishes in the dishwasher. For a minute Martin got to thinking about his sister. If only she liked baseball, moving to the city would have been easier. They could play together and hang out like pals. Then it wouldn't matter so much that the other kids wouldn't let him play. But Jeannie always got bored whenever Martin tried to teach her to play. Maybe things would be different when she was older, Martin thought as he walked out onto the front porch.

All at once he heard the slap of sneakers on the sidewalk. It was Barry Welton.

"Hi, Barry!" he called.

"Hi, Marty," Barry answered. "Taking it easy?"

Martin nodded. "Wait a minute, Barry," he said. "I'll be right back." Martin ran into the house.

He got the bat and glove and brought them out. "Here," he said, swallowing a lump in his throat. "Take them back. They'll never let me play baseball around here!"

Barry frowned, but then a grin came over his face. "Hey, kid. Don't go acting like that or you'll never play ball! Got a ball?"

Martin said, "Yeah, but —"

"Get it. We'll play a little catch."

Martin went inside again, full of excitement this time, and got the ball.

"Let's go out to the side of the house," Barry suggested, "so we won't be throwing toward the windows."

Martin thrilled at the expert way Barry caught the balls, pulling his hands down and away with the ball. He tried to do the same. They played catch for about fifteen minutes, and then Barry said he had to go. In the meantime Jeannie had come out to jump rope on the porch. After Barry left, Martin still wanted to play.

"Jeannie," Martin said, "how about throwing the ball to me in the backyard? I'll bat. Then after a while you can bat."

"Okay."

Martin was grateful that she was willing, even though she didn't like baseball that much. She wasn't such a bad sister after all.

They had more room in the backyard. But it was not as much fun as Martin had hoped. Each time Jeannie threw the ball, he swung and missed.

At first he joked with Jeannie about throwing him wild pitches. But then missing the ball four, five, six times in a row got under his skin. He was growing warm all over, and he

knew it was because he was getting anxious and mad.

"Martin," said Jeannie, "what's the matter? Can't you even hit it?"

"I could if you threw it right!" Martin said angrily.

"Well, who wants to play this boring game, anyway?" Jeannie yelled back. She threw the ball down in the dirt.

Martin threw his bat down, too.

They heard Mom's voice calling from the house: "Jeannie! Martin!"

They ran into the kitchen. Their mother held the keys to the car in her hand.

"If you two can sit in the backseat without fighting, maybe we could take a trip to the movies," she said.

"Yeah!" They said it almost together, their faces lighting up like Fourth-of-July sparklers.

"Okay," she said. "Get washed and dressed."

The movie was a comedy. They laughed all

the way through it. Not once did Martin think about baseball.

Martin was in bed before he remembered the bat he had left outside. He rushed out the side door and searched all around the spot where he was sure he had left it. But it was nowhere around.

The bat was gone!

4

First thing the next morning, Martin searched the backyard again. The bat could have rolled behind one of Dad's rosebushes, or into the higher grass that grew close to the wire fence, he thought. But he still could not find it.

Martin felt sick. He would not have minded so much except that the bat was a gift from Barry. And now it was gone. What could have happened to it? Did somebody take it?

He couldn't stop thinking about the bat as he wandered up the street. Then he saw some boys playing with a tennis ball. One of them was Rick Savora.

Rick was about eleven or twelve — bigger than Martin. He stood with his legs spread apart and held a bat on his shoulder, waiting for another boy to pitch him the tennis ball. Farther down the street was a third boy, waiting to chase the ball in case Rick hit it.

Martin waited to see what Rick would do. Rick, he remembered, was one of the boys at the park yesterday. He looked as if he might be the best player of them all.

Rick swung at the ball and hit it down the street past the pitcher. He dropped the bat and raced around the squares of cardboard they were using for bases.

Then Martin noticed the bat. It had rolled a little way as Rick had thrown it and then had stopped. Martin's heart pounded like mad. He started to walk down the street.

One of the boys saw him. "Here comes that Allan kid!" he cried out.

Rick stood on second, his hands on his knees. When he heard the boy shout, he rose and scowled at Martin.

"What do you want?" he yelled.

Martin didn't answer. He looked at Rick and then again at the bat. The more he looked at it, the more it looked like the one Barry had given him.

The boys muttered in low tones among themselves. One of them walked off the street. Rick picked up the cardboard piece that was second base, got the bat, and walked off the street, too. The catcher followed him.

All three gave Martin dirty looks and went up on the porch of a red brick house nearby.

A hurt look crept into Martin's eyes, and an ache filled his throat, wanting to turn into tears. He spun on his heel and ran all the way home.

He met Jeannie in front of the house, bouncing a rubber ball up and down on the sidewalk.

"Rick Savora's got my bat!" Martin exclaimed.

Jeannie's eyes widened. "Did you ask him for it?"

"No. I didn't have a chance. He and some other kids went into his house when they saw me coming."

Jeannie's lips tightened. "Let's go to his house and ask him for that bat," she said, determined.

"What if he won't give it to me?" Martin asked.

"Then we'll tell Dad about it."

Martin shook his head. "No. I won't tell Dad anything. I don't want the kids to think I'm a baby."

"Well, let's go anyway. If it's your bat, he must have stolen it, and we'll make him give it back."

Together they walked to Rick Savora's house. Rick answered Martin's knock. He scowled when he saw who his callers were.

"You were playing with my baseball bat," Martin said. "I want it back."

"You're crazy!" Rick snapped. "I haven't got your bat!"

"Yes, you have. You were playing with it on the street just a little while ago. I saw it."

Rick's eyes blazed with anger. "Just a minute!" he snarled.

He went inside and soon returned with a small yellow bat.

"There! Is that your bat?"

Martin looked at it closely. "No," he said. "But that isn't the one you were playing with."

"You're crazy!" Rick said again. "You must've been seeing things!"

He slammed the door so hard the wood panels shook. Jeannie and Martin turned and stared at each other.

"He's lying," Martin said as they started back up the street. "I know he's lying!"

5

A little after dinnertime, Martin was sitting on the porch when a car stopped in front of the house. "Hey, son!" called the driver. "Want to come to the park and play ball?"

Martin recognized Coach Jim Cassell. He walked slowly down the porch steps and toward the car.

Then he saw Rick Savora sitting in the car next to Mr. Cassell. Rick didn't look at him.

Martin felt a tightening in his chest. "I — I don't think so," he said. "I don't think I want to play baseball."

"What? I thought you *wanted* to play."

Martin shrugged. He didn't want to say that he wouldn't play because Rick was on the team. He couldn't tell the coach that Rick had stolen his bat and then lied about it.

Coach Cassell flashed a smile. "Got a glove?"

Martin nodded. "Yes."

"Then get it. We're going to have a team in the Grasshoppers League, and since you're one of the boys in the neighborhood, maybe we'll have room for you on the team."

"A Grasshoppers League?" He frowned. "What's that?"

"A league we have here. There are six teams in it. Each team plays two games a week during the summer vacation. The winning team gets a free banquet and goes to see a World Series game. It's something worth shooting for. Don't you think so?"

"WOW!" Martin's face brightened. "I'll say it is!"

The coach's smile broadened. "Now you want to come along?"

"You bet! Wait! I'll run in and get my glove!"

At the field, Coach Cassell had two of the tallest boys choose sides. Rick Savora chose for one side, and a red-haired boy named Lennie Moore chose for the other. Lennie picked Martin for his team. Then the coach flipped a quarter to see whose side would bat first. Rick called "heads" and won the toss. He chose to bat last.

Coach Cassell told the boys which positions they were to play, then called out the hitters for Lennie's team. Martin noticed that Rick was playing shortstop. He wondered what position the coach would let him play. He had never thought about playing in a league! And to have a chance to see a World Series game! What a wonderful thing that would be! Even his parents had never seen a World Series game!

"Okay, Martin! Your turn to bat!"

He sprang from the bench, surprised that his name was called so soon. The second one!

He picked up one of the bats and went to the plate. His heart hammered. He got into position beside the plate, tapped it a couple of times with the bat, and waited for the pitcher to throw. The next thing Martin saw was the ball coming at him and over the plate.

He swung. Missed!

Coach Cassell was acting as umpire. "Strike!" he said. Then he turned to Martin: "Get a little closer to the plate, Martin. You're too far from it. And keep your feet farther apart."

Martin tried to do what the coach said. Again he waited for the pitch. He swung! Missed again!

Sweat beaded on his forehead. He was growing more nervous by the second. If he didn't get a hit, they would see he wasn't any good. And then they wouldn't want him on the team.

The third pitch came in. He had to hit it

now. He was thinking that if he had his own bat, the one Barry had given him, it would have been a cinch. This bat was too heavy.

The ball was in there, straight as an arrow. Chest-high. He swung!

He heard the ball hit the catcher's mitt. The bat, following through on his swing, spun him almost all the way around.

"Strike three!" said Coach Cassell.

6

The day of the first game in the Grasshoppers League came quickly. Too quickly for Martin. He dreaded having to play in front of a crowd. In every practice he had been hardly able to hit the ball.

His dad had given him a pep talk. He had even taken him to a professional game, to show him that even major leaguers strike out sometimes.

But it didn't make Martin feel much better. What he really needed was his own bat back.

He was sure that with his own bat he would hit.

Martin's team, the Tigers, was playing the Indians. Coach Cassell put Martin out in left field — because Martin was good at catching fly balls, he said.

The Tigers were up first, and Kenny Stokes was the leadoff batter. He hit the second pitch for a blooping fly to the shortstop.

Then Martin walked to the plate. The bat felt heavy in his hands. He hadn't been able to find one among the team's bats that fitted him as well as the one Barry had given him.

The pitch came in, but he wasn't ready for it. He let it go by. "Strike!" yelled the umpire.

"Come on, Martin!" He heard the coach's voice from the bench. "Hit it when it's in there!"

He ticked the next one. It went sailing back over the catcher's shoulder, striking the backstop screen.

"You're feeling it!" he heard the coach shout.

He got ready for the third pitch. With an 0 and 2 count on him he was in a tough spot. He wished the coach had not put him second in the batting order. Everybody would expect too much from him.

The pitcher wound up, then threw. But the ball came in too wide. Martin let it go by.

"Ball!" said the umpire.

Now the count was one ball, two strikes. He felt a little better. Again the pitch. It came in straight and a little low, but Martin swung at it. And missed!

"Strike three!" boomed the umpire.

Martin dropped the bat and walked sadly back to the bench. He knew what everybody was thinking.

Jackie Barnes was up next. He hit the ball to the left of second base for a single. Rick Savora followed him and hit the first pitch for

a double. Next, Chuck Sterns hit a grounder through short, scoring Jackie and Rick. Then Chuck got out trying to steal second.

When the Indians came to bat, they scored three runs, edging ahead of the Tigers, 3 to 2.

Larry Munson was on second base when Martin came to bat again. It was the third inning. If he got a hit now, Larry might score to tie the game.

The pitch came in. It was a little high, but it didn't look bad. Martin cut at it. *Crack!* The ball looked as big as a balloon as it floated through the air toward the pitcher. Martin threw down the bat and started running slowly toward first.

"Run, Martin!" Coach Cassell shouted. "Run!"

But the ball dropped into the pitcher's hands. Sadly, Martin turned and headed back for the bench.

Nobody said anything to him, but he heard the coach say, "Artie, play catch with

36

somebody. You're going in in place of Martin next inning." He looked up at Martin. "Martin —"

"I heard you, Coach," Martin said. Then he turned to Rick, his eyes hard as steel.

"If you'd give my bat back to me, I could hit that ball!" he cried bitterly. "You're a thief, that's what you are! You stole my bat!"

7

Rick's face paled, and his mouth opened as if he were going to say something. But Martin was already running off the field, carrying his glove.

He wondered what Jeannie and his mother and father would say when he came home early. Well, what could they say? They could see that he couldn't hit the ball. It was only right that he had been taken out.

He saw a fat, chubby-legged little boy run out into the street, chasing after a blue-and-red rubber ball. He wasn't more than three years old.

A car whizzed around the corner, its tires screaming on the pavement. Martin stared at the car, then at the little boy. Terror took hold of him. The little boy wasn't paying any attention to the car!

Suddenly the loud cry of a woman reached Martin's ears. "Gary! Gary, get back here! Watch that car!"

There was fear in her voice. Martin saw her run toward the street. "Gary!" she screamed again.

The little boy did not move. Realizing that the car would not be able to stop in time, Martin sprinted out into the street, picked up the boy, and snatched him out of the way.

The car's brakes squealed, its tires leaving twin black marks on the street behind it. Then it stopped, and a man looked out of the window, his face ghost-white.

"Man!" he exclaimed. "That was close!"

"It sure was!" said Martin with a shudder. The little boy started to cry, and Martin carried him to his mother. He saw that their backyard faced his backyard.

"Thank you!" the boy's mother said to Martin. "Thank you so much!" Her face was white as she bent and picked up her little son.

Then a tall, brown-haired man ran out of the house, followed by a freckle-faced boy, a year or two younger than Martin, who Martin recognized as Freckles Ginty. Shakily, the woman told her husband what had happened. The husband looked at Martin.

"That was quick thinking, son," he said. "We're very grateful to you for going after little Gary like that. You deserve some kind of reward."

Martin smiled. "That's all right," he said. "I'm glad I came by when I did."

He went home, feeling good at the man's words.

He had hardly been home five minutes when a soft knock sounded on the door. He knew it wasn't Dad or Mom. They wouldn't knock.

Wondering, he went to the door and opened it. It was Freckles Ginty. He held a bat in his hand, and he lifted it up to Martin.

Martin's eyes went wide. It was his missing bat!

8

At the ball field the next afternoon, just before practice, Martin approached Rick. He felt nervous and ashamed.

"Rick, I — I'm sorry that I said you had my bat. I got it back yesterday. Freckles Ginty had taken it out of my yard."

Rick frowned. "Why?"

"No good reason. He just saw it there and took it. Anyway, he brought it back and apologized."

Rick shrugged his shoulders. "Okay. You got it back. Maybe you can hit that ball now."

Martin heard the sarcasm in his voice and wondered if he and Rick would ever be friends. Rick was tough in a way, but everybody seemed to like him.

"Did you go in their house?" Rick said suddenly.

"No."

"You should see some of the things Mr. Ginty makes out of wood. Have Freckles show you sometime."

"I will!" Martin smiled.

On Thursday afternoon they had another Grasshoppers League game, this time against the Bears. Martin took Artie's place in the third inning, and when it was time to bat he wasn't nervous anymore. The bat felt just right in his hands. He felt good. He waited for the pitcher's throw — and hit the very first pitch for a single!

The crowd yelled. He could hear Coach Cassell's voice: "Thataboy, Marty! I knew you could do it!"

In the sixth inning, an important moment came, with the score 8 to 6 in the Bears' favor. The bases were loaded. Martin was up to bat again. A hit could tie the score. A good long drive could win the ball game.

The pitcher stepped onto the mound, glanced at the runner on third, then threw. Martin swung.

Crack! Like a white bullet the ball shot over the shortstop's head. Martin dropped the bat and sprinted to first base. The ball hit the grass halfway between the left and center fielders. Both boys ran as fast as they could after it, but it bounced on beyond them!

One run scored! Two! Three! Then Martin crossed the plate. A home run!

Martin's hit had won the game: 10 to 8.

The bat was lucky, all right. Martin kept on

hitting the ball in every game. Coach Cassell placed him third in the batting order, just before Rick. At the end of their fifth game, Martin's batting average was .453 and Rick's .422. Barry Welton came to see Martin play whenever he wasn't playing himself. And of course, Jeannie and his mom and dad never missed a ball game.

He even got on Jerry Walker's cable TV sports program. How long had he played ball? Jerry asked him. What was his batting average? What did his mother and father think of his playing baseball?

Finally Jerry mentioned his bat. "Coach Cassell tells me you have a bat you won't let anybody else use," he said. "You must think a lot of that bat, Martin," he added, smiling.

"I sure do," Martin answered. "It's my lucky bat."

When August came, the Tigers and the Bears were tied for first place, and the boys were growing more excited by the day. They kept talking about the World Series game that they might see.

"We've got three more games to play," Coach Cassell said. "We must win two out of those three. If we win, we're in!"

They started playing the first of the three games. For the first two innings neither team scored. Then the Bears picked up two runs.

In the fourth inning the Tigers scored two runs to even it up. It stayed that way till the first half of the sixth. Larry was first batter and got a single, a nice one over first base. Kenny Stokes walked. Then Martin came up, and everybody cheered.

He swung at the first pitch. Missed! The next one was a ball. The third was in there. He swung hard and hit it — a neat single — but something terrible happened: the bat broke in two! He held one piece in his hand. The other piece was flying out across the ground toward third base!

9

Martin didn't know what to do. Without his bat he was sure everything would be the way it was before. He wouldn't be able to hit again, and the coach wouldn't let him play anymore.

There were only two games left to play. The Tigers had won one. They had to win one more. If they lost the next two games, their chance of seeing a World Series game was gone.

"It isn't the bat, son," his father said to him. "It's you. You've got it in your head that you can't hit with any other bat, but you're wrong. Just try again. Try again, Martin."

Martin wished that it would rain on Friday, the day of their next game. But it didn't.

The Tigers were up first. The first two batters flied out. Then Martin came to the plate. He took three cuts and struck out.

"Never mind that, Marty," the coach said. "You'll hit it the next time."

Martin didn't say anything. When the next time came, he would strike out again, he thought. The coach would find that out himself. Maybe he didn't believe the bat made a difference, but it did. There must be something about that bat. That he'd struck out his first time up with another bat proved it. How could anybody say it didn't?

The game ended 7 to 4 in the Bears' favor.

At one o'clock Saturday afternoon, Martin was still home. The game was scheduled to start at exactly one-thirty.

His father appeared at the living-room door. He frowned. "Martin! Why aren't you at the baseball field?"

Martin's heart started to pound. "I'm not going to the game," he said.

"Why not?"

"Because I'm no good. I can't hit. I can't field. The coach just lets me play because I *used* to be good."

"That's no way to talk, son," his father said. "The coach lets you play because he knows you're good. You're just thinking about that bat again. And you're wrong. I wish I could make you understand that."

The doorbell chimed and his dad went to answer it.

"Martin!" he called. "Someone to see you!"

Martin walked across the room to the door, then stopped. It was Freckles Ginty.

"Hello, Martin. I've got something for you."

From behind his back Freckles pulled a bat. Martin stared. It was exactly like the one he had broken!

His mouth fell open. "Where — where did you get it?"

"It's the same one you broke," Freckles said, grinning. "My father glued it together again for you."

10

"Strike one!" yelled the umpire.

Martin rested the bat again on his shoulder. He wasn't worried about having a strike called on him. This was his fourth trip to the plate. Besides hitting a long fly ball that the center fielder had caught in the third inning, he had two hits. One was a single, the other a triple.

Mr. Ginty has sure paid me back for saving his little boy on the street that day, Martin thought. Imagine fixing up the bat so it's like new again! He sure is a wonderful man!

The pitch. "Ball!" boomed the umpire. "One and one!"

The score was 7 to 5. The Tigers were ahead. There was a man on first. It would not hurt to knock in another run. The team that won this game won the trip to the World Series.

"Come on, Marty!" the gang on the bench shouted. "Come on, kid! Hit that apple!"

Then he heard his dad. "Drive it, Marty!"

The pitch came in. He swung. *Crack!* The ball sailed out between left and center fields! Martin dropped the bat and ran. He touched first, second, third — and didn't stop until he crossed home plate!

A home run!

"Hurray, Marty!" everybody roared.

Rick caught him and shook his hand. "Thataboy, Marty! Thataboy!"

"Nice going, Marty!" exclaimed Coach Cassell. "Guess we'll be heading for the World Series game!"

Martin's heart beat so fast he thought it would leap right out of his shirt.

The Bears lost hope after Martin's long clout. They didn't score any more runs. The Tigers won, 9 to 5.

Jeannie ran to her brother right after the game and hugged him. Then came his father and mother. Then Barry Welton.

"You'll be a big leaguer one of these days, Martin," Barry said.

Martin beamed, then shook his head. "I can't use this bat all my life," he said, holding up the bat. "It'll be too small for me when I grow up!"

Then another voice broke in, a soft voice that Martin had heard only once before. "Martin, I have a confession to make. I hope you'll forgive me if I tell you."

Martin looked around. It was Mr. Ginty,

Freckles's father. Martin was puzzled. "What do you mean, Mr. Ginty?" he said.

"I made that bat, Martin."

Martin stared. His heart flew to his throat. "You — you mean it isn't the one I used to have? The one that Barry gave me? The one I busted in two?"

"No, it isn't. I don't think I could ever fix that other one up so that you could use it again. This is a brand-new bat. I made it myself — just for you."

Martin swallowed hard. He put out his hand. Mr. Ginty shook it. "Thanks, Mr. Ginty!" Martin said. "Thanks a lot!"

Then he turned to his dad. He could barely see him through the tears that blurred his eyes. His father smiled back.

"You see? It wasn't the bat, was it, son?" he said.

Martin shook his head.

It was just him.